MR. ZUMPO'S AMAZING ZOO

OF UNUSUAL ANIMALS

WRITTEN AND ILLUSTRATED BY

MR. WOLF

For Cassidy Denness

CHAPTER ONE

'Haha! Look at that monkey's bum. It's bright red!' laughed Raj, pointing at the baboon in the enclosure.

His sister giggled and started shouting, 'Red bum! Red bum!'

'That's what I'm going to call you!' Reya's brother teased. 'From now on, I'm gonna call you Red Bum! Haha!'

In reply, Reya poked out her tongue and blew a loud raspberry at Raj.

'Come on you two,' said their dad. 'Why don't you stop arguing and go and fetch your old man an ice cream. I suppose you could have some as well… if you want some that is…'

'Ooh yes please! Yes please!' shouted his kids, now completely forgetting about the baboon with the red behind.

Their dad gave them some coins and they hastily ran through the zoo towards the ice cream stand.

'Come straight back!' their dad shouted after them. 'And don't talk to any strangers!'

1

Raj and Reya loved coming to the local zoo to see all the animals. They sometimes felt sorry for the animals being locked up, but they knew the animals were looked after and that most of them wouldn't survive in the wild.

Reya's favourites were cute creatures like otters, meerkats and penguins, but Raj preferred the big animals like elephants and bears.

As they ran down the path, Reya said, 'Look at that giraffe!' The children stopped running and walked over to the enclosure.

Raj said, 'It's got the longest neck of any giraffe I've ever seen! Look at how high its head is!'

Reya added, 'I bet he can see all the way to India!'

The giraffe slowly chewed some leaves from the top of a tall tree, completely ignoring the children.

'It must take a while for his food to reach his stomach,' observed Raj.

'Eh?' asked his sister.

'Well, with such a long neck, just think how long it must take for the food to travel down it!'

'Oh yes!' Reya replied. 'Hey, that means that when a giraffe is sick, the vomit must take ages to travel up its throat!'

'Urggh!' said Raj. 'That's disgusting!'

They tried to see if they could spot any other giraffes with necks longer than the one they had been watching, but they couldn't find any.

'Giraffes are brilliant, aren't they?' Raj exclaimed.

'Yeah! I love giraffes!' agreed Reya.

'Huh!' said a voice that didn't belong to Reya or Raj. The children turned around to see who had spoken.

The voice continued, 'Giraffes! What utterly boring and mundanely ordinary animals! Huh!'

Standing before Raj and Reya was a short and plump man. He was wearing a cape and a top hat, and he was holding a walking stick. He also had a long moustache which he was twiddling between his chubby fingers. 'Giraffes are so uninteresting,' he carried on. 'Don't you agree?'

'No, I do not!' replied Raj. 'Giraffes are great! They're magnificent animals!'

'Oh, you think so, do you?' the man replied.

'Yeah!' Reya chipped in. 'Giraffes are brilliant!'

'My, my,' said the man. 'I suppose you think hippos and kangaroos are interesting too!'

'Well of course!' Raj said.

The man shook his head and ambled over to the other side of the path. He looked at the rhinoceroses and proclaimed, 'Oh, rhinos! How terribly, terribly mundane!' Then he wandered past the lions' enclosure and said, 'Huh! Lions! There's nothing quite as boring as a lion!'

Raj and Reya were following him. 'Why don't you like lions?' Raj asked. 'You don't seem to like *any* animals!'

'Oh, I absolutely *love* animals, dear boy!' the man said with a sudden energy about him. He grinned a large toothy smile and continued, 'I just think this zoo has the poorest examples. Why, they don't even have a Ginger-Spotted Woo-Woo Bird, let alone a Rapsical Otrocillator!'

The man carried on walking slowly down the path, as the children followed behind him. 'A Radical Otter what?' said Reya, giggling. 'There's no such thing!'

'Nor a Ginger-Spotted Woo-Woo Bird!' added Raj. 'You've made them up!'

The man replied, 'I can assure you that I have not. Why, Woo-Woo Birds and Otrocillators are actually rather common, if you know where to find them. And I really can't believe this zoo doesn't have a Trombonial Pig-Fish.'

Reya nudged her brother and whispered, 'They're not real creatures, are they?'

'No, of course they're not real!' replied Raj.

'I can assure you they are!' the man said firmly, tapping his walking stick on the ground. 'Why, if you were to visit *my* zoo, you would find not only Woo-Woo Birds and Trombonial Pig-Fish, but many other much more marvellous animals!'

'You have a zoo?' asked Reya.

'Indeed I do!' the man said proudly. 'I own the most incredible zoo in all the world!'

'Well, where is your zoo?' asked Raj.

'Aha!' the man answered dramatically. 'Only people who are invited are allowed to know how to get to my zoo! I can't have just anybody visiting such a marvel of zoological specimens!'

'His zoo doesn't sound very logical to me,' Raj whispered to his sister.

'What's your zoo called?' asked Reya.

The man tapped his walking stick three times and announced, 'Mr. Zumpo's Amazing Zoo of Unusual Animals!'

He had announced it with such flair, that Raj and Reya found themselves getting excited. 'Are you Mr. Zumpo?' Raj asked.

'Indeed I am,' said Mr. Zumpo. Then he added, 'Well, it was nice to meet you. I hope you

6

have fun with your lions and tigers and whatnot, but I really must be on my way.' Mr. Zumpo then turned around and began to walk away, a little quicker than he had been walking before.

'Wait!' cried Raj. 'Couldn't we visit your zoo sometime?'

'Ooh yes!' Reya said excitedly. 'Please Mr. Zumpo! Couldn't we come and see your Woo-Woo Birds?'

Mr. Zumpo stopped and turned around. 'Hmmm....' he mumbled, whilst twiddling his moustache. 'Well, I suppose you do deserve to see more than the boring animals this zoo has to offer. Hmm... Very well. Come with me, and you will discover the most unusual animals in all the world!'

CHAPTER TWO

'But we can't go to your zoo *now!*' Raj told Mr. Zumpo. 'Our dad will already be wondering where we are, and we have to buy some ice creams.'

Mr. Zumpo replied, 'Well, I'm afraid that my zoo cannot be travelled to by conventional means. The only way of getting there is by accompanying me, so I'm afraid it's now or never. Although I can guarantee you that you'll still be able to find ice cream at my zoo. And it's the most delicious ice cream in all the world! Still, if you need to get back to your father...'

'Oh, I want to go to his zoo!' Reya said to her brother. 'Why don't we go and ask dad if we can?'

'Hm, I don't think dad would like us going off with strangers,' replied Raj.

'Oh, I'm not all that strange, am I?' asked Mr. Zumpo, grinning.

Reya giggled and said, 'Well, actually you are *very* strange!'

Raj looked embarrassed at his sister's

remark, but Mr. Zumpo just laughed and said, 'Yes, I suppose I am rather strange! After all, there is no one quite like me, and nowhere quite like my zoo.'

'Sorry Mr. Zumpo,' said Raj, 'but we really can't go now. We don't have the time.'

'Aha!' replied Mr. Zumpo. 'Well, actually, I might be able to help out in the time department.'

'Whatever do you mean?' asked Raj.

Mr. Zumpo answered, 'My zoo is so precious, that I have had to hide it in a very secret place. I have therefore devised a time-warp-security-wall around it.'

'A what?' the children asked.

'It exists in a place just slightly askew of the normal laws of science, so that no one but me can locate it. It will take just a jiffy to get there, and when we return, it will be as though no time has passed at all.'

'What?' exclaimed Raj. 'You mean we can visit your zoo and still come back to this moment in time? Come off it!'

'It's a lot simpler than it sounds,' replied Mr. Zumpo. 'All one has to do is harness the power of the Quantum Quacker-Crocker's eggs.'

'Quantum what?' giggled Reya.

'Quantum Quacker-Crocker,' Mr. Zumpo repeated.

'Quantum Kacker-Quocker?' said Reya. Mr. Zumpo shook his head, so Reya tried again: 'Quantum Quacka-Wacca-Wocka? Quantum Clocker-Whacker?' - but she couldn't get it right.

Mr. Zumpo then said, 'Come on!' and he pushed a red button on the top of his walking stick and tapped the stick on the ground three times.

The ground below began to swirl around in circles and in no time at all, there was a spiral slide below their feet. 'There we are!' proclaimed Mr. Zumpo. 'The entrance to my zoo! All we have to do is slide down. You can come for an hour or two, and then I'll bring you back here to this very moment!'

There were plenty of people around, but nobody seemed to have noticed the new tunnel that had manifested (because Mr. Zumpo knew that it's often best to hide miraculous things in plain view if you don't want them to be noticed).

'Come on!' cried Mr. Zumpo with a cheerful smile, and he slid away down the spiralling tunnel. The ground then swirled around Reya and Raj, and before they knew it, they were also sliding down the spiral slide towards the Amazing Zoo of Unusual Animals.

At the end of the long slide, Mr. Zumpo and the children fell into a massive beanbag. Then Mr. Zumpo climbed down a rope ladder to the ground and Raj and Reya followed.

'Here we are!' exclaimed Mr. Zumpo. 'This is my amazing zoo!'

They were stood before some incredibly large doors which were coloured bright pink. Above them was a neon sign proudly displaying the name of the zoo. There were also lots of fruit trees and colourful flowers surrounding the walls of the zoo.

'Come on!' said Mr. Zumpo, and he walked towards the large doors. When he reached them, he knocked with three sharp raps of his walking stick and the doors opened.

Mr. Zumpo then ushered the kids inside and the large pink doors closed behind them.

'You will have never seen anything like these animals!' Mr. Zumpo told the children. 'You'll find no ordinary creatures *here*!'

'Well, what about that then?' asked Raj. He was pointing at the only animal that could be seen. 'It's just a cow!' said Raj, indicating the cow.

'Not at all!' replied Mr. Zumpo. 'That is a Woc.'

'What's a Woc?' asked Reya.

'A Woc is very much like a cow,' Mr. Zumpo informed them, 'only, its front is where its behind should be and its behind is where its front should be.'

'But then it would look just like a normal cow!' said Raj.

Reya added, 'It *is* a normal cow!'

'You really should look at things in more detail,' replied Mr. Zumpo. 'Look closely and you'll see its legs appear to be round the wrong way.'

On closer inspection, it could be seen that this animal was indeed a Woc, and not a cow.

'Anyway, that Woc isn't part of the show,' said Mr. Zumpo. 'I only have it because it produces the most delicious milk in the world. It's why my ice creams taste so good.'

They carried on down the path and came across a strange animal in an enclosure. 'What's that?' asked Reya.

Mr. Zumpo replied, 'That's a Blue Gnu that moos.'

They passed the bright blue gnu and heard it moo.

'That certainly is an unusual animal,' said Raj.

'My boy,' replied Mr. Zumpo. 'You've not seen anything yet!'

CHAPTER THREE

'Here we are!' Mr. Zumpo announced, as they stopped by the first cage.

Raj and Reya peered into it. They could see an old tyre and a bowl of water, but there didn't seem to be any creature in the cage at all.

'I can't see anything,' said Raj.

'Well of course you can't,' Mr. Zumpo replied. 'This is an Ignonian Invisible Wibble Beast, and as everyone knows, Ignonian Invisible Wibble Beasts are invisible.'

'Well, how do you know it's there if you can't see it?' Reya asked.

Raj added, 'I don't think there's any such thing as your invisible beast. You've made it up!'

'Have not,' said Mr. Zumpo. 'Watch.' He pointed at the bowl of water in the cage. It was quickly disappearing with a loud sucking noise. Then came the sound of a burp.

Raj and Reya looked through the bars of the cage and saw footprints appearing in the sandy ground.

'There really is an invisible beast in there!' cried Reya, grinning with excitement; but she also felt a little afraid.

'I told you so,' said Mr. Zumpo. He began walking, so the children followed him. He stopped in front of a large enclosure and said, 'Next we have a Ping-Pong Popperphant.'

The creature looked a little like an elephant, only its ears were long curly antlers, its tail was made of feathers and its tusks had little umbrellas on the ends. It was also coloured bright yellow.

'What a very odd animal!' said Reya.

The Ping-Pong Popperphant began swaying its long trunk from side to side before pointing it into the air. Then, with a quick motion, the Popperphant popped dozens of ping-pong balls out of its trunk. One hit Mr. Zumpo on the nose. PONK!

'Ow!' cried Mr. Zumpo.

Raj and Reya quietly giggled.

'Come, come, we have much to see!' Mr. Zumpo said, rubbing his nose and suddenly striding onwards down the path. 'Over there, you can see the Ferocious Curly-Furred Fleur Bird, and down that path is the Muzzled Moon Mouse, but we don't have time to see everything. We'll have to give the Humpbacked Gobble-Blugs a miss too. Come on, I want to show you my Long Necked Jiffaroo. If you think giraffes' necks are long, you'll have to think again!'

They arrived at the pen of the Long Necked Jiffaroo. Reya and Raj bent their heads backwards as much as they possibly could so they could try to see the head of the Jiffaroo which was hidden in the clouds above.

'Its neck is approximately four miles long,' Mr. Zumpo informed them. The creature really did have a most absurdly long neck.

'Next,' said Mr. Zumpo, turning around and briskly walking down the path, 'we have the Sneeze-A-Lot Green-Snotted Snuffler. But we need to be prepared. Here, take these.' He picked up a couple of umbrellas next to the Snuffler's cage and handed them to Raj and Reya. 'Watch out for its snot!' Mr. Zumpo said.

The Sneeze-A-Lot Green-Snotted Snuffler was the size of a bear. Its body was furry, but the fur was covered in a glistening, gloopy, green substance. The Snuffler's head had one eye, three ears, sharp pointy teeth and a long snout. The snout had slobbery green gunk hanging from its nostrils, and the gunk constantly dripped down onto its furry, slimy body.

The one-eyed snotty Snuffler looked at Mr. Zumpo and his companions. Then it began making a sound: 'Atchh... atchh... atchh...'

'Look out!' said Mr. Zumpo.

'ATCHHH... ATCHHH... ATCHHOOOOOO!'

The Sneeze-A-Lot Green-Snotted Snuffler had just sneezed an enormous sneeze. Green, slimy snot had shot out of its snout at a hundred miles per hour, covering the umbrellas that Mr. Zumpo and the children were shielding themselves with.

Then, 'ATCHHH... ATCHHH...' the sound came again. 'ATCHHOOOOOOOOOOOO!' This time, the Snuffler's snotty sneeze was so strong that it blew the umbrellas away, and coated Raj, Reya and Mr. Zumpo in horrible, snotty, greeny mucus!

'Urrrrgh!' the children complained.

'Oh dear, oh dear,' said Mr. Zumpo. 'It would seem the Snuffler's in a particularly sneezy mood today.'

'ATCHHH... ATCHHH...' The noise began again.

'Come on! Quick!' said Mr. Zumpo. He ran away down the path and Raj and Reya quickly followed after him.

When they came to a halt around a corner, Reya said, 'Urghh! I'm covered in horrible snot!'

Mr. Zumpo replied, 'We'll soon fix that. Let's go and see the Welsh Bell Whale!'

After a few minutes, they arrived at a very large swimming pool. Something could be seen lurking at the bottom.

'Is that the whale down there?' asked Raj.

'It is,' answered Mr. Zumpo. Then he tapped his walking stick beside the pool and the Welsh Bell Whale splashed out of the water and swam towards Mr. Zumpo and the kids.

Reya was trying to wipe Snuffler snot off of her face, but it was such a sticky substance, that there was no getting rid of it.

'The Bell Whale will have us washed in no time,' said Mr. Zumpo, and he tapped his walking stick again.

The Welsh Bell Whale looked very much like a normal whale, except that it was bell-shaped and was striped red and yellow. Suddenly, water shot out of the spout on the top of its head. The water showered Raj, Reya and Mr. Zumpo and it wasn't long before they were clean and snot-free.

'Brrr!' said Reya, shivering. 'I'm all wet now!'

Mr. Zumpo replied, 'Don't worry!' and he tapped his walking stick once more.

The Welsh Bell Whale then blew a warm jet of air out of its blowhole, aiming it right at Raj, Reya and Mr. Zumpo. In no time at all, they were all completely dry.

'You really do have some unusual animals,' said Reya.

'I know,' replied Mr. Zumpo.

CHAPTER FOUR

Raj asked, 'Where did you get all these animals from, Mr. Zumpo?'

'Oh, from many different places. I have spent my life dedicated to the collection of strange and exotic creatures and have travelled to all sorts of incredible places to find them. Look here, we have a Horse-Hog.' Mr. Zumpo pointed towards an animal that was shaped like a horse, but it was completely covered in long pointy spikes. Its body, its legs, its neck and its head were all spikier than a porcupine.

'And in the distance,' said Mr. Zumpo, you can see a Soapy-Bubble Blow-Duck.'

Reya and Raj looked at the bird which was blowing large soapy bubbles out of its beak.

'What's that over there?' Raj asked, pointing at another very peculiar looking creature.

It had seventeen eyes on the top of its head, it had two upside down pointy ears on its chin, and its mouth looked just like a banana.

The odd creature's body was a large, round, furry ball. It bounced over to Raj, Reya and Mr. Zumpo.

'What a silly creature!' laughed Reya. 'What's it called?'

'Clive,' answered Mr. Zumpo.

'I didn't mean its name,' said Reya. 'I meant: what sort of animal is it?'

'It is a Clive,' replied Mr. Zumpo. 'They're not actually too rare. It's quite easy to find Clives if you want to. You can catch them when they bounce south for the winter.'

They walked on and passed a Grumpy Bubble-Gum Chawooga. The animal looked depressed and angry as it leered at Raj and Reya.

'What a strange creature!' said Raj. 'Its body looks like it's made out of stringy chewing gum. And look! Parts of it keep blowing up like bubbles and popping!'

'And what's that over there?' asked Reya, pointing at another unlikely animal.

'Ah! That is an Octopussycat,' stated Mr. Zumpo.

The creature's main body did look very much like a cat's, but its head looked more like that of a fish. The Octopussycat also had eight long, oily tentacles, which seemed to have tied themselves up in knots. The creature was trying to untangle itself, but it seemed to be having trouble.

'Shouldn't you help it?' Raj asked Mr. Zumpo.

'No, no! Never interfere with an Octopussycat. They're always getting themselves tied up.'

Then Mr. Zumpo added, 'Come, let us visit the Big Blue Tit.'

Blue tits are of course generally considered to be cute little songbirds. When somebody sees a blue tit or hears its song, their heart is usually filled with joy. However, upon encountering the Big Blue Tit, one feels quite the opposite.

'ARGHHHHH!' cried Reya and Raj at suddenly seeing the enormous bird looming over them. The shadow of the blue tit engulfed them all.

The Big Blue Tit was in fact the biggest bird in existence. It was as large as three tower blocks high and two ASDA superstores wide. It was the biggest creature that Raj and Reya had ever seen, and its immense size was very frightening.

The Big Blue Tit seemed to be scowling at them. Then, its large sharp beak suddenly snapped right at them, as it screamed a loud, 'Tzeeeeeeeeee!' which deafened Reya and Raj.

The children ran away, covering their ears, as Mr. Zumpo ambled behind them, saying, 'I thought you'd like my Big Blue Tit.'

'Oh but Mr. Zumpo,' said Reya, 'it's so big! I've never seen such a frightening creature!'

Mr. Zumpo looked somewhat bemused at their reaction. 'Come on then,' he said, 'let's take you to see something nicer. Over here, we have a Cutesy-Tootsy Cuddler.'

They wandered over to a cage which contained the unusual animal. The Cutesy-Tootsy Cuddler was the size of a small kitten, and three times as furry! It had two large pleading eyes, and one was slightly skew-whiff, which just made the Cutesy-Tootsy Cuddler even cuter.

Raj and Reya sighed, 'Ohhhhhhh!' for a very long time. Then the Cutesy-Tootsy Cuddler suddenly brandished its teeth and roared at them loudly: 'RAAAARRRR!' Then it swung its sharp claws towards Raj and Reya, which made them jump back with fear.

'I should have warned you,' said Mr. Zumpo. 'It's teething at the moment. It's been in a bad mood all week.' Then he started walking quickly down the path, so the children once again followed him.

'What's that smell?' Reya asked.

'Poo! Yes, what is that?' asked Raj.

Mr. Zumpo said, 'I can't smell anything.'

'It's coming from that direction,' Raj replied, pointing down a path.

'Ah yes, I can smell it now!' said Mr. Zumpo. 'That's the smell of the Super Pooper Stinky Pong Beast. He's only a couple of miles away.'

The stink grew stronger. 'Cor!' complained Reya. 'It smells like dirty nappies, whiffy drains and sick!'

Raj began coughing as he said, 'Poo! It reeks worse than Reya's socks!'

'Oi!' said Reya, and she nudged her brother in the ribs.

'Would you like to visit the Super Pooper Stinky Pong Beast? He does smell a bit, but he's worth seeing,' said Mr. Zumpo.

'Cor! No thanks!' Reya replied, holding her nose.

CHAPTER FIVE

'Who looks after all the animals?' Raj asked Mr. Zumpo as they walked down the path. 'Surely you can't run this zoo all by yourself.'

Mr. Zumpo replied, 'Indeed I can't. I have zookeepers for that. Hm, they must all be on their lunch break at the moment. Would you like to meet them?'

Raj and Reya said that they would, so they followed Mr. Zumpo down a track and arrived at an old barn. There were loud voices coming from behind it. 'Here we are,' said Mr. Zumpo as he led the children round the back of the barn.

Sitting around a makeshift table were several, what appeared to be, chimpanzees in flat caps, arguing and laughing. They were playing cards and smoking disgustingly horrible smelly cigars.

'Ha!' said one chimpanzee, as he gathered up the stakes. 'I win again! You'll have to do better than that, lads!'

'Those apes can talk!' Raj said to Mr. Zumpo, astounded.

'Why, of course,' replied Mr. Zumpo. 'These are Inner-Mongolian Short-Haired Speaky-Speak Champinzees.'

'Don't you mean *chimpanzees*?' asked Reya.

'No, I do not!' replied Mr. Zumpo.

The zookeepers all stopped playing their game when they saw that Mr. Zumpo had arrived.

'Alright Mr. Zumpo,' said the ape that had won the card game. 'I sees you's brought some visitors.'

'Yes, I've come to introduce them to you.' Mr. Zumpo then reeled off the zookeepers' names to Raj and Reya. 'This is Mugsy. That is Glugsy. Over there are Bugsy and Jugsy. And in the corner are Dugsy,

Wugsy and Slugsy. Hm, but we seem to be missing one. Where's Lugsy?'

Just then, Lugsy came running towards them. ''ere, guv,' he shouted to Mr. Zumpo. He arrived at the barn, out of breath and said, ''ere! The Ignonian Invisible Wibble Beast has disappeared!'

'Don't be so stupid, Lugsy,' said Mugsy. 'The Invisible Wibble Beast always looks like it's disappeared.'

'Nah, mate. I mean it's escaped.'

'But 'ow do you know if you can't see it?' asked Mugsy.

Lugsy replied, ''cos I opened its cage door to feed it and it leapt out and trampled me underfoot! That's 'ow I know!'

'Oh,' said Mugsy. 'I see.'

'Oh dear!' cried Mr. Zumpo. 'We can't have an Ignonian Invisible Wibble Beast on the loose! No, no! Quick, zookeepers, go and find that animal at once!'

'But guv,' said Mugsy. 'We ain't finished our lunch yet.'

Mr. Zumpo started getting angry, which made Reya and Raj a little afraid of him. Mr. Zumpo shouted at the zookeepers, 'Get off your behinds and find my Invisible Wibble Beast NOW, or I'll lock you all up in cages and you'll become exhibits!'

The champinzee zookeepers all mumbled and moaned. They slowly got to their feet, whilst scratching their armpits and stubbing out their horrible, stinky cigars.

'Now!' cried Mr. Zumpo. 'There is no time to lose!'

'Alright, alright,' muttered Wugsy. 'Keep your hair on.'

Then the zookeepers all disappeared to search for the invisible beast.

'Is the Invisible Wibble Beast dangerous?' Raj asked.

'No, no,' assured Mr. Zumpo. 'But nevertheless, we can't have it gallivanting around.'

'But how will the zookeepers find it?' Reya asked. 'After all, it is invisible!'

'Well, they had better find it...' said Mr. Zumpo, starting to sound angry again. Then he coughed and said in a lighter tone, 'Now, what do you say we go and see the rest of my unusual animals?'

They were now standing before what looked very much like a new-born Labrador puppy. 'Ohhh, it's so cute!' said Reya, delighted.

'Look at how small it is!' added Raj. Then he asked Mr. Zumpo, 'What's so unusual about a puppy?'

'Aha!' replied Mr. Zumpo. Keep watching the dog and you'll see!'

The new-born puppy suddenly looked like it was a few weeks old. It had grown considerably in less than a minute. It slowly grew even larger until, just a few minutes later, it was a fully-grown adult Labrador dog barking its head off.

'Woah!' cried Reya and Raj.

Then the dog started to look older and older until, after only a few more minutes, the Labrador before them was a weak, shaking thing.

'Come on,' said Mr. Zumpo, leading Raj and Reya away. 'I find that most children don't like seeing the last two minutes.'

'Eh?' asked Raj, looking behind him, as Mr. Zumpo hurried them on.

THUD! The Labrador had just dropped dead behind them.

'Oh, it's died!' cried Reya, who was twisting her neck round to see. She started crying.

'Hm, maybe I shouldn't have brought you to see that one,' said Mr. Zumpo. 'Children are often disturbed by the short lifespan of the Growth Accelerating Labrador.'

For just a brief moment, Mr. Zumpo grinned, but neither of the children noticed.

'You mean those animals only ever live a few minutes?' asked Raj.

'Yes,' replied Mr. Zumpo. 'But it's quite natural for them, of course. It's not anything to be sad about.'

Reya didn't agree. She was wiping tears from her eyes.

As they wandered down the path, Raj said to Mr. Zumpo, 'You mentioned that other children had seen your Growth Accelerating Labrador. Do you have a lot of children visiting your zoo?'

'Oh, you know,' answered Mr. Zumpo, 'from time to time.' Then he said, 'Now, we have a very fine specimen of an unusual animal over here. Come on, let's visit the Wurly Wurlitzer Whistleroo.'

CHAPTER SIX

The Wurly Wurlitzer Whistleroo could be heard long before they reached it.

Its loud noise was like a wheezy penny-whistle accompanied by an out of tune organ.

They arrived at its pen and saw that the Whistleroo was an oblong creature covered in long curly hair from head to toe; if it could be said that a Whistleroo had a head and toes.

It grinned a large smile the size of a piano keyboard. Its teeth were white and black and it suddenly opened its mouth wide and let out another loud screechy organ sound.

Reya and Raj were giggling at the strange creature. Then it whistled – only the whistle hadn't come from the animal's mouth. No – the whistle had shot out of the Whistleroo's bottom. 'WHEEEEEEWW!'

'Ha, ha!' laughed Reya. 'It whistles from its bum!'

Mr. Zumpo said, 'That's nothing. I've somewhere got a Car Alarm Caterpillar which emits a really annoying alarm noise from its nostrils. We can never find it until it suddenly starts wailing at two in the morning.'

Once more, Reya and Raj followed Mr. Zumpo, who now seemed to be in an incredible hurry. He was almost running to the next enclosure.

'Here we have a Dinosnore!' declared Mr. Zumpo.

The Dinosnore was sound asleep and snoring, as was the habit of Dinosnores.

'It looks like a small T-Rex!' Raj observed.

'Yes, it does somewhat,' agreed Mr. Zumpo. 'But it's much less frightening. After all, it spends ninety-nine per cent of its life asleep.'

The Dinosnore just lay there snoring, so they went over to the next enclosure.

'Here we have a Kanga-Two,' declared Mr. Zumpo. 'This is one of my finest unusual animals! There aren't many Kanga-Twos about these days!'

The Kanga-Two looked rather a lot like a kangaroo, only there were two. One was upside down on top of the other, but they were joined together so that actually it was only one creature.

As the Kanga-Two hopped towards them, a joey fell out of its upside-down pouch and landed on the ground. The Kanga-Two nearly bounced right on top of it, but then it just picked up the joey and came over to Mr. Zumpo and the kids.

'Hello!' said Reya and Raj, stroking its nose.

Suddenly a loud noise like, 'Pt-bt-chee pt-bt-chee...' frightened the Kanga-Two away.

'That'll be the Beatbox-Bunny,' said Mr. Zumpo. He walked over to a cage behind them. 'He's always frightening the Kanga-Two.'

The Beatbox-Bunny started beatboxing a grooving funky beat, all with the sole aid of its mouth.

Reya and Raj started tapping their feet in time.

'Do you like it?' asked Mr. Zumpo, although he didn't seem to want an answer. He was already hurrying away. 'I find the Beatbox-Bunny's beats rather repetitive myself.'

Raj said to Reya, 'I think the Beatbox-Bunny's great.'

'Yeah,' she agreed.

'Come, come!' shouted Mr. Zumpo. 'We really must be getting on! Come on, you little blighters.' He was grinning, but he did look very impatient, so Reya and Raj caught up with him.

'Next,' said Mr. Zumpo, pointing at a cage that seemed to have little in it besides a three-seater sofa, 'we have the Furniture Chameleon. It can change into absolutely any item of furniture.'

Raj and Reya watched as the sofa transformed into a dining table. Then it became a sideboard before finally opting to be a hat stand.

'That's not actually an animal, is it?' asked Reya.

'Of course it is!' stated Mr. Zumpo, as he rushed them onwards.

'Phwahahahahorhaha!' came a loud laugh out of nowhere.

'What's that?' asked Reya.

They approached the animal's cage as Mr. Zumpo said, 'This is the Guffawing Goggle-Woff.'

The animal once again began guffawing 'Phorhahahahahorhorhaha!' as it writhed around on the ground.

Next to it was a small chick-like bird who started giggling, 'Teeeheeeheheteehe.'

'That's a Giggle-Chick,' Mr. Zumpo informed them.

Reya and Raj began giggling themselves, and as the Guffawing Goggle-Woff and the Giggle-Chick continued to laugh and titter, Reya and Raj laughed even more. Laughter, of course, is known to be highly infectious.

'Come, come!' ordered Mr. Zumpo, striding onwards. 'Over here we have a Gravity-Defying

Gopher!' The gopher was indeed defying gravity: he was hovering three feet above the ground.

'And here we have a Peppermint Hippo,' said Mr. Zumpo, moving on quickly. The hippopotamus was coloured light green and it had the strong scent of peppermint.

'He's great!' said Reya. 'I'd love to have a Peppermint Hippo.'

Raj replied, 'I don't think it would fit in our house.'

'We could keep it in the bath,' Reya said.

Mr. Zumpo interrupted them. 'This next animal is one of only two left in the whole world. I'm rather proud to have it in my collection.'

They approached a cage. 'This is a Posh-Me-Posh-Ewe,' Mr. Zumpo informed them.

The animal looked like a sheep with two heads. It was wearing two monocles, a tiara and a diamond necklace. The Posh-Me-Posh-Ewe seemed to be inspecting a copy of the Financial Times. Then it began muttering to itself, 'Fraffle-fraffle-fruff-righly-rot-wot.'

Mr. Zumpo said, 'It does tend to think that it's terribly posh. And it will eat nothing but caviar and drink nothing but champagne! It costs me a fortune!'

The two headed posh sheep turned a page of the Financial Times and muttered, 'Fraff-fraff-fruff-rot-wot-tot.' Then it walked on all fours to a bowl of champagne and drank the lot in one go. The Posh-Me-Posh-Ewe then rang a bell.

One of the zookeeper champinzees (it was Dugsy) came running as fast as he could to be of service to the Posh-Me-Posh-Ewe.

Dugsy was dressed in a butler's suit (although the arms of the jacket were too short, he wasn't wearing a shirt, and he still had his flat cap on his head). He said to the Posh-Me-Posh-Ewe, 'At yer service. What can I do for ya?'

The Posh-Me-Posh-Ewe pointed at its bowl and mumbled, 'Fraff-fruf-mur-sham-wot-tot.'

So Dugsy filled up the bowl with more champagne.

Five times more, the Posh-Me-Posh-Ewe asked for more champagne; but then it did have two heads.

The animal started swaying from side to side and then fell, face first - SPLAT! - into a large mound of caviar. It burped a smelly breath of alcohol and then fell asleep.

'Is it alright?' asked Reya.

Mr. Zumpo replied, 'Yes, yes. It's the normal behaviour of a Posh-Me-Posh-Ewe. It goes through this routine every day. It really does cost me a fortune...'

Dugsy started taking off his butler suit, as Mr. Zumpo asked him, 'Have you found the Ignonian Invisible Wibble Beast yet?'

'No guv,' replied Dugsy. 'We don't know where to look.'

'Oh you useless champinzees! Go and find my Wibble Beast NOWWWW!' Mr. Zumpo had suddenly gone red with rage. He was angrily hopping up and down on the ground, whilst waving his walking stick in the air.

Dugsy just mooched off, mumbling under his breath some rude words about Mr. Zumpo.

Reya whispered to Raj, 'Mr. Zumpo does seem to have a short temper, doesn't he?'

Before Raj could answer, Mr. Zumpo was smiling a large smile and saying, 'Come on. Let's go and get some ice cream!'

CHAPTER SEVEN

'CLACKER-KLOCK-CLACKER-KLOCK-KLACK...'

'What is that annoying noise?' asked Reya.

Mr. Zumpo replied, 'That is the mating call of the Clacton Klaxon Cluck.' They passed the creature's cage. It looked something like a six-foot-tall purple furry chicken with a rotating head.

'Come on, the ice cream's just down here,' said Mr. Zumpo, as they passed more unusual animals.

These included:

- A Pickled Plicker Picker, which Reya and Raj would find hard to describe.
- A Spitty-Gob-Gob, which had long sticky drool hanging from every part of its slimy body, and which hastily spat at Reya and Raj as they rushed past.
- The Terrifying Torture Troll, whose red eyes were all that could be seen.
- A Humpitty-Mumpitty Camel, who instead of having one or two humps, had little humps all

over its body and head, like it had a severe case of mumps.

- The Door Mouse, who had a door where his body should be. He kept opening it and trying to climb through, but with no success.
- The Long-Tongued Quick-Flick Licker, which had an extremely long, slobbering tongue. It poked its tongue out between the bars and stretched it all the way to Reya's ear, which tickled Reya and made her scream and laugh simultaneously.

- The Mushroom Moose, which looked just like a moose, except that it was covered in mushrooms.
- The Bling-A-Ding Glisterer, which was sparkling with gold.
- The Greater Spotted Pox, which looked like a spotted chicken.
- The Proxy Fox which looked just like a badger.
- The Odd-Shaped Pig, which was - of course - a pig that was very oddly shaped.

There were also:

- A Vincunian Vustler.
- A Lopsided Lobster Dog.
- A Big Eared Bobble Beast.
- A Long Nosed Nobble Beast.
- A Scritchy-Scratchy Nitcher-Natcher.
- A Philosophical Penguin.
- A Four-Horned Hopeless-Puss.
- A Speedy Swift Swoosher.
- A Lesser Spotted Rotter Otter.
- A Lipsticked Dipstick Duck.

- A Tenacious Toad.
- A Bat Cricket.
- A Fifty-Fingered Finkler-Fuss.
- A Bendy Rubbery Pubber-Bub.
- A Well-Mannered Mongoose.
- A Bad-Mannered Tues-Goose.
- A Zip Mouthed Moth.
- A Greedy Bankerian.
- A Sideways Scuba-Fish.
- A Man-Bat.
- A Wonky Worm.
- A Polaroid Bear.
- A Tickler-Tock.
- An Upside-Down Ditsy-Wink.

And:

- The Hundred-Hairy-Legged Death-Spider, which was four times the size of Reya and Raj.

As they rushed past, the Death-Spider poked out several of its hairy legs from between the bars. The legs tried to grab Raj. One caught his ankle which made him fall over and scream: 'ARHHHH!'

Mr. Zumpo turned around and saw that the big spider was trying to drag Raj into its cage. 'Stop that! Stop that!' he shouted. 'That boy's not for you!'

Mr. Zumpo then ran over to the Hundred-Hairy-Legged Death-Spider's legs and bashed them with his walking stick until the spider let go of Raj.

The Death-Spider retreated into a corner of its cage and whimpered.

Raj was trying to put on a brave face, but it was clear that he'd been very frightened. Reya was also looking rather afraid.

Mr. Zumpo said, 'Huh! That Death-Spider nearly got you! That would have been no good at all! No, no!' Then he addressed the children with, 'Come on, come on, the ice cream is just over here.' He smiled a large grin and took Raj and Reya over to a small ice cream van.

Mr. Zumpo got inside the van. From behind the counter he said, 'All these ice creams are made from delicious Woc milk! You'll have never tasted ice cream so good! Now, let's see – what would you like? We've got Swirly-Whirl Strawberry, Triple Chock-Full Chocolate, Raspberry Ripple-Plop, Very

Vanillary Vanilla, Creamy Cracking Coconut Crunch, Fizzy Whizz Sure-Bet Sherbet Lemon, and Tutti-Frutti-Sweeti-Tweeti.'

Reya decided to have a Triple Chock-Full Chocolate ice cream. Raj plumped for a Raspberry Ripple-Plop.

'There we are,' said Mr. Zumpo, as he handed them their ice creams, whilst grinning a large grin.

'Mmm!' and 'Yum!' came the kids' replies, as they started eating their ice creams hungrily.

'Aren't you having one?' Reya asked Mr. Zumpo.

'No, I don't care too much for ice cream,' he replied.

As Raj and Reya devoured their ices, Raj said to Mr. Zumpo, 'Why did you keep going on about how delicious the ice cream was if you don't like it yourself?'

'Oh, because the children always love it so much,' replied Mr. Zumpo.

Reya suddenly stopped eating and yawned an ever so loud yawn.

'Don't you want to finish your ice cream?' Mr. Zumpo asked her, smiling.

Reya yawned again and said, 'No... It's very nice... but... oh, I am... so... very... tired... all... of... a... sudden...'

Raj looked very tired too. He also began yawning a very loud yawn, and he dropped his ice cream to the ground. 'I... don't feel so good...' he said weakly.

Then Raj and Reya collapsed unconscious to the ground.

Mr. Zumpo grinned. Then he laughed an evil laugh and said, 'Ha! That was easy! Children really are so stupid! They fall for my poisoned ice cream every time! Ha, ha, ha, ha, ha!'

CHAPTER EIGHT

Mr. Zumpo was now walking around the zoo, searching for his zookeepers.

'Where have those champinzees got to?' he said to himself. 'They better have found my Ignonian Invisible Wibble Beast or I'll lock up the bally lot of them!'

He stopped at a fork in the path and decided to turn left. Soon, Mr. Zumpo was near the entrance of his zoo. He passed by the Woc.

'Haha!' laughed Mr. Zumpo. 'I do like making ice creams from the milk of the Snooze-Drug Woc!' (Which was the animal's full species name.)

Mr. Zumpo strode down the path, calling out, 'Mugsy? Lugsy? Dugsy? Anybody? Where are you filthy champinzees?'

Suddenly, BANG! Mr. Zumpo had just walked into something that wasn't there. It had crushed his nose and made it bleed. 'OW! What the...' he began to ask, but he soon realised that he'd just bumped into the Invisible Wibble Beast.

'Mugsy!' yelled Mr. Zumpo.

Mugsy, Dugsy and Wugsy then appeared in the distance and ambled towards their boss.

'Quick! Quick!' shouted Mr. Zumpo.

The zookeeper champinzees ever so slightly quickened their pace.

'The Invisible Wibble Beast is here!' Mr. Zumpo shouted.

'Oh. Right,' said Mugsy, as he and his colleagues arrived by Mr. Zumpo. Then Mugsy asked, 'Well, where is it?'

'I don't know!' replied Mr. Zumpo. 'But it was just here! It bashed my nose!'

'Oh yeah!' laughed Mugsy, looking at Mr. Zumpo's red, bleeding nose.

The other champinzees started laughing too.

'It's not funny!' Mr. Zumpo replied angrily. 'Now find my Wibble Beast!'

Mugsy scratched his head and said to Dugsy and Wugsy, 'What do ya reckon lads? I s'pose we could try and fish it out with some of its favourite food.'

'Yes, yes!' said Mr. Zumpo. 'Set a trap for it!'

'Yeah, alright,' said Mugsy. 'Only we're out of mouldy broccoli. That's its favourite, that is. But I s'pose we might be able to tempt him with a bit of stale cauliflower.'

'Do it right away!' shouted Mr. Zumpo. He turned on his heel and walked off. Then he looked back over his shoulder at Mugsy, Dugsy and Wugsy who were standing around scratching their heads.

Mr. Zumpo shouted, 'If you don't get a move on, I'll lock up the lot of you!'

So, the champinzees started laying a trap for the Ignonian Invisible Wibble Beast.

Meanwhile, Raj and Reya were coming to. Their heads felt ever so fuzzy. They opened their eyes and blurrily saw dozens of children standing around them.

Reya and Raj were in a large, damp, dingy, dirty cage. 'Uh! What happened?' asked Raj.

'Where are we?' added Reya.

'You've been caught by Mr. Zumpo of course,' said a girl. 'Just like all of us!'

'I knew we shouldn't have gone off with a stranger!' said Raj. 'Oh, how foolish of us! We're prisoners!' He felt bad that he had put his sister in danger more than he felt scared for himself.

'What a rotten trick!' said Reya. 'And I thought Mr. Zumpo was such a nice man!'

'He must have drugged our ice creams,' Raj stated.

The girl in the crowd of children said, 'Yes. That ice cream makes you fall asleep and then you end up here. We've all been through it. We all thought we were having a great time seeing his unusual animals, only to end up here in this horrible cage!'

'The dirty rotter!' said Raj. Then he asked the girl, 'How long have you been here?'

'I've been here for four days,' she replied. 'But some of the kids have been here for weeks.'

A boy piped up, saying, 'I've been here two whole weeks now. Mr. Zumpo will come along every couple of days and take some of us away. Then he brings new kids along, like you.'

'But what does he want us for?' asked Raj. 'Are we to be part of the zoo?'

'No, no,' replied the boy. 'He feeds us to the Child-Eating Crack-Cruncher.'

CHAPTER NINE

Mugsy, Dugsy, Wugsy and Lugsy were hiding around a corner. Mugsy was holding the end of a long piece of string that was attached to a cardboard box, which was propped up with a stick.

Under the box was some stale cauliflower – the bait for catching the Ignonian Invisible Wibble Beast.

'It's taking its time,' said Mugsy. ''ow long d'you reckon we'll 'ave to wait?'

'Dunno mate,' said Wugsy. 'Still, it beats 'aving to clean out the Super Pooper Stinky Pong Beast's cage. That's what I was s'posed to be doing now.'

'Cor! Poo!' said the other champinzees.

Mugsy said, 'I hate cleaning out the Super Pooper Stinky Pong Beast's cage.' His mates all agreed with him that it was a horrible, disgusting job.

Dugsy started dealing out cards for a game, when suddenly Mugsy shouted, 'OH!'

'What is it?' the champinzees asked.

'The stale cauliflower in the trap! It's gone!' answered Mugsy.

'Eh?' said the others, looking over at the trap.

Wugsy said, 'How did that happen? Where's it gone?'

Mugsy replied, 'Oh! Don't you see? The Ignonian Invisible Wibble Beast ate it! We didn't see it, so we weren't able to trap it!'

'Oh… yeah… right…' came the grumbling replies of the others, as they scratched their armpits and heads, wondering how they were going to catch the Invisible Wibble Beast now.

'Zumpo won't be happy if we don't catch it, y'know,' said Lugsy.

'No, he will not,' agreed Mugsy. 'Bloomin' Zumpo! He's always giving us a hard time. He has no respect for the working class, that's his problem! He doesn't appreciate how hard we works…'

The other champinzees all mumbled in agreement, and they soon started airing their gripes about their employer, now completely forgetting about the Ignonian Invisible Wibble Beast.

As night began to fall, Mr. Zumpo climbed into his Claw Crane (which was a vehicle and not an unusual animal). He put his key in the ignition and started it up. Then he drove down a track towards the cage where he kept all the children.

'Blinking horrible children!' Mr. Zumpo muttered to himself as he drove. 'I really can't stand the little blighters. Having to bring them here and put up with their excitement all the time – huh! Just to feed the belly of that big Child-Eating Crack-Cruncher! Honestly... that animal does take up a lot of my time and effort...'

Mr. Zumpo turned the headlights of the Claw Crane on. It was almost pitch black now. He continued to mumble, 'I wonder... maybe I should get rid of the Crack-Cruncher... I could get a good price if I sold him... But then he is my prime specimen... Ah, well – there are plenty of children locked up to keep him going this week... And, ooh, I do love to hear the bones of those kids being snapped in half by the gigantic sharp teeth of the Child-Eating Crack Cruncher... Hm, yes, I'd miss that if the animal wasn't around...'

Mr. Zumpo stopped having a conversation with himself as he approached the cage with all the children in it.

'Look!' said a boy in the cage. 'Zumpo's coming!'

The children all looked at the crane that was pulling up beside their cage. The kids then started running around (as much as they could in the cage's cramped conditions) and they began screaming.

'What do we do?' asked Reya amongst the confusion.

'I don't know,' shouted Raj.

Then the roof of the cage suddenly slid open, by way of a remote control that Mr. Zumpo was using.

'Ha, ha, ha, ha!' laughed Mr. Zumpo. 'I really do hate children.'

The claw of the Claw Crane was like one of those that you use at the amusements to try and grab a plastic troll or a teddy bear. Mr. Zumpo set it into action and the claw crashed down into the cage.

The children who had been there the longest knew exactly what to do: hang on to the bars or scramble away from the claw as much as possible.

Reya and Raj, however, were complete novices at this game, so before they knew what was going on, the claw had grabbed both of them, and three other children, and it was now hoisting them up into the air.

'Ha, ha, ha, ha, ha!' laughed Mr. Zumpo, as he drove the crane down a track; the claw gripping the children tightly.

Not before long, amongst the darkness of the quiet night, the kids could hear a loud: 'ROOOOOAAARRRRR!'

The five children shuddered, as Mr. Zumpo shouted to the gigantic Child-Eating Crack-Cruncher that had roared, 'There, there, my pet. I know you're hungry. Not long now. I have some lovely children for you to crunch. Don't you worry!'

'ROOOOAAAAAARRR!' came the sound again.

Some huge, sharp white teeth that presumably belonged to a Crack-Cruncher's mouth, suddenly appeared in the black night. The children all screamed, as Mr. Zumpo parked his crane next to the Child-Eating Crack-Cruncher's cage.

CHAPTER TEN

'Raj! What'll we do?' Reya asked her brother. 'Mr. Zumpo's going to feed us to that horrible Crack-Cruncher!'

Raj tried to say something, but the hungry sound of the Child-Eating Crack-Cruncher drowned his words.

'ROOOOOAAAAAARRRRR!'

'There, there,' said Mr. Zumpo to the beast, 'I've got some lovely prime condition children for you. And they're fresh too!'

'ROOOOOOOOAAAAAARRRRR!' came the reply of the Crack-Cruncher.

Mr. Zumpo reversed the crane a little and began straightening it up, so that he could move the claw over the top of the Crack-Cruncher's cage.

The Crack-Cruncher bashed the cage and roared again, as Reya, Raj and the other three children were hoisted over the bars.

'ARRRGHHHH!' screamed Reya. 'We're going to be eaten alive!'

Raj and the other kids then also screamed, as the claw began to loosen its grip – so they would drop straight down into the Child-Eating Crack-Cruncher's drooling mouth.

'Hahahaha!' laughed Mr. Zumpo, as he pushed down the lever that controlled the claw.

Then, all of a sudden: BASH-WOOSH! Mr. Zumpo was suddenly flying out of the crane, through the air. CRASH! He landed on the ground and lay there unconscious.

'What happened?' Raj said, looking at Mr. Zumpo.

The claw that held the kids still dangled over the mouth of the Crack-Cruncher. The animal roared again, frustrated that its food was just out of reach.

Then the crane started reversing, all by itself.

There was no one in the driver's seat, but the wheel was being turned, levers were being pulled, buttons were being pressed, and the Claw Crane was doing some rather nifty manoeuvres.

'What's going on?' asked Reya.

'Who's driving the crane?' Raj said.

Soon enough, the children were no longer above the mouth of the Crack-Cruncher. They were being lowered to the ground to safety. Then the claw opened and let them go.

'Are you alright?' Raj asked his sister.

'I think so,' said Reya.

In fact, all of the children were safe and well. They ran away from the cage of the beast, and then stopped to look back at what was going on.

The crane was now picking up Mr. Zumpo with its claw. As it gripped Mr. Zumpo tightly, he woke up and began shouting and swearing.

The crane then hoisted the claw over the top of the cage. The Crack-Cruncher roared.

Mr. Zumpo screamed, 'AAAARRHHHH! What's happening? What's happening? Put me down!' He looked at the crane and saw that no one was driving it. That made him scream even louder.

Then the claw let go of Mr. Zumpo.

He fell into the huge mouth of the Crack-Cruncher and the beast's sharp, saliva-drenched teeth began chewing him up. Mr. Zumpo's screams died away. Now all that could be heard was the sound of crunching bones.

'Hm,' thought the Child-Eating Crack-Cruncher, as it swallowed Mr. Zumpo. 'That was tasty! Better than children!'

Mugsy, Dugsy, Wugsy, Lugsy and the other champinzees had heard the commotion and were now wandering towards the crane and the children who were huddled together in a corner.

'Eh up,' said Mugsy as they arrived. 'Where's Zumpo?'

Raj explained how he had been eaten by the Crack-Cruncher.

'Really?' came the replies of the champinzees. 'You mean it? Zumpo's been eaten?' They all looked hopeful and began to smile.

'Yes!' replied Reya. 'That crane seemed to have a mind of its own. It saved us and fed Mr. Zumpo to the Crack-Cruncher.'

The champinzees all began cheering and shouting hooray. Then they started dancing around in circles and singing, 'Zumpo's been eaten! Zumpo's been eaten! Hoorah!'

Reya, Raj and the other three children were now sitting with the zookeeper champinzees beside their barn. Slugsy had made a fire and Dugsy had made tea for everybody. After a while, the kids had calmed down from their ordeal of nearly being eaten.

'I must say,' said Mugsy. 'I didn't think the Crack-Cruncher liked to eat anything but children. But, oh, how good it is that Zumpo's gone! He was a wicked man and he treated us terribly y'know!'

The other champinzees all mumbled in agreement.

'Well now you can run the zoo by yourselves!' said Raj.

The champinzees all started agreeing that it was a brilliant idea.

'Yeah,' said Mugsy. 'And we'll treat the animals more kindly than Zumpo ever did too! He didn't care about their welfare – he just cared about his collection! Huh! Blooming Zumpo!'

Dugsy said, 'Yeah. And we should sell that Child-Eating Crack-Cruncher too. I don't think it's right that it eats children, y'know!'

'And adults!' said Wugsy. 'Or maybe Zumpo was an exception.'

'Anyway,' said Lugsy, 'we should get rid of the Crack-Cruncher.'

The champinzees all began agreeing again. Then Wugsy said, 'So what will we call the zoo now?'

Mugsy suggested that they call it Mugsy's Amazing Zoo of Unusual Animals. Dugsy thought Dugsy's Amazing Zoo of Unusual Animals had a better ring to it, and needless to say, all the other champinzees thought their own names sounded best.

They began arguing, until Raj interrupted them and said, 'Can't you decide on that later? There are more important things to get done first! There are other children locked up, and we all need to get home!'

'Oh. Yeah. Right,' said the champinzees.

Reya then said, 'But I still don't understand what happened. How did that crane move all by itself? How did it save us?'

The champinzees began laughing. Reya huffed and said, 'Huh! I don't see it's anything to laugh at!'

Mugsy said, 'Sorry – it's just that the answer to your question is obvious to us.'

Reya, Raj and the other children looked blankly at Mugsy.

Mugsy said, 'It was the Ignonian Invisible Wibble Beast that saved you!'

'Oh!' cried the children.

Dugsy said, 'That Wibble Beast hated Zumpo. It didn't want to be locked up, you see. So it must have seen Zumpo about to feed you to the Crack-Cruncher and decided to intervene.'

'But how can an Invisible Wibble Beast drive a crane?' Raj asked.

'Oh, Wibble Beasts are very clever, y'know,' Mugsy answered. 'And it's got its freedom now. We won't be locking that animal back up. It's saved us all!'

CHAPTER ELEVEN

After a short while, Mugsy had unlocked the other children from their cage and they were now all standing around the champinzees, asking questions and shouting, 'We want to go home!'

'Alright, alright!' Mugsy shouted to make them quiet. 'Calm down!'

Raj said, 'How do we get home Mugsy? Do we have to climb back up the spiral slide?'

'No, no, no,' said Mugsy. 'That will have disappeared as soon as you set foot in the zoo.'

'Oh!' said Raj, as the other children started mumbling.

'What's needed to get home,' said Mugsy, 'is Zumpo's walking stick!'

'But Mugsy,' said Reya, 'where is his walking stick? Was he holding it when he was eaten by the Crack-Cruncher?'

Mugsy's face fell. 'Oh... Oh dear....' he said. 'I don't know. But if we don't have the walking stick, you can't get home!'

'Oh no!' all the children cried.

'We'll have to look for the walking stick,' said Raj, taking control. 'We need to be absolutely certain as to whether it was eaten by the Crack-Cruncher or not. We'll have to wait until daylight to search though.'

The children all looked disappointed, but they agreed that Raj's plan was a very good one.

One of the children then said, 'But what'll we do if we can't find it? What if the Crack-Cruncher really has eaten it? How will we get home?'

Raj answered, 'We'll have to wait for the Crack-Cruncher to digest it.'

'What?' said half of the children, not understanding what Raj meant.

'What?!!' said the other half of children, knowing exactly what Raj meant.

'We'll have to wait for the Crack-Cruncher to poo...' Raj explained, making it clear that it would be someone's job to wade amongst the poo and find the walking stick.

'Eurghhhhh!' came the replies of the children.

Reya asked Mugsy, 'Is there really no other way of getting home?'

'Afraid not,' answered Mugsy.

Just then, a very strange thing happened. Mr. Zumpo's walking stick was floating through the air towards them. It then hovered above Raj's head before dropping into his hands.

'What the....?' Raj asked, as the other children gasped.

'Ha, ha, ha,' laughed Mugsy. 'That good ol' Invisible Wibble Beast! Thank you, thank you, wherever you are!'

There was a strange noise and a sharp gust of wind. It would seem the Invisible Wibble Beast had just gone on its way.

'It must have saved the walking stick for us!' shouted Raj. 'What a good Wibble Beast!'

'So how do we use it?' Reya asked Mugsy.

'Just tap the walking stick three times,' he replied, 'and press that red button on the top. At the bottom of the slide, you will each return to wherever it was you came from – and remember: no time will have passed at all.'

'OK,' said Raj. 'Thanks Mugsy, and all of you.'

The other children all began thanking the champinzees, which made the zoo keepers blush and scratch their armpits.

'Ready?' Raj asked the children.

'YEAH!' came the reply.

Raj tapped the walking stick three times and pressed the red button. Sure enough, the ground began to swirl. Then a spiral slide tunnel appeared.

Raj and Reya decided to let the other children go first, so one by one, they all zoomed down the spiral.

At last, only Reya and Raj were left. 'Thanks again,' they said to the champinzees. Then Raj added, 'And make sure you look after those animals!'

'Will do,' said Mugsy.

Reya, followed by Raj, then slid down the spiral slide and arrived back at their local zoo.

The champinzees, meanwhile, returned to their debate about what to now call the zoo of unusual animals.

'We're back!' said Raj, smiling.

'Hooray!' said Reya.

It felt like they had been away for a very long time and it seemed extremely strange to now be standing on a path in their local zoo, with other people ambling around them.

'Look at that hippopotamus!' they heard a small child say. 'I've never seen such a strange animal!'

Raj and Reya smiled at each other.

Then Reya said, 'Hey, we never did see Mr. Zumpo's Woo-Woo Birds!'

'Come on,' said Raj, 'let's go and find dad. And I don't think we should go off with strangers ever again!'

After just a few minutes, they spotted their dad and ran towards him at a great speed. They crashed into him and started hugging him tightly.

'My word,' said their dad, 'what's come over you two?'

'Oh, it's so good to see you!' said Reya, as she hugged him.

'What are you two playing at now?' asked their dad.

Reya and Raj finally let go and looked at their dad with beaming faces.

Their dad said, 'Don't tell me you've forgotten the ice creams!'

Raj and Reya looked at each other. Then Raj replied, 'I don't think we want any now.'

OTHER BOOKS BY MR. WOLF

Terry The Time Travelling Tortoise

The Top Secret Cheese

www.booksforchildren.wix.com/mrwolf

Printed in Great Britain
by Amazon